TRICKY COYOTE TALES

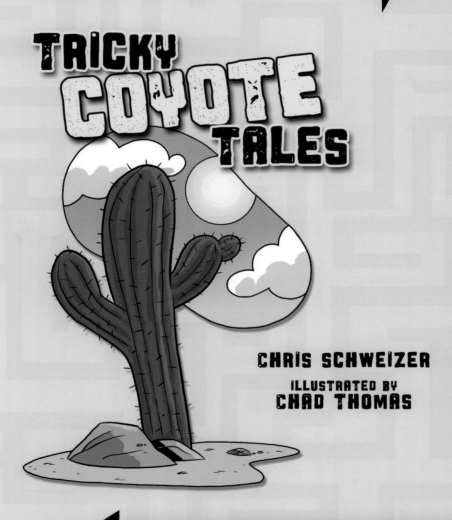

CHRIS SCHWEIZER

ILLUSTRATED BY
CHAD THOMAS

GRAPHIC UNIVERSE™ • MINNEAPOLIS • NEW YORK

Story by Chris Schweizer

Illustrations by Chad Thomas

Coloring by John Novak

Lettering by Grace Lu

Copyright © 2011 by Lerner Publishing Group, Inc.

Graphic Universe™ and Tricky Journeys™ are trademarks of Lerner Publishing Group, Inc.

Graphic Universe™
A division of Lerner Publishing Group, Inc.
241 First Avenue North
Minneapolis, MN 55401 U.S.A.

Website address: www.lernerbooks.com

Main body text set in CC Dave Gibbons Lower 14/22.
Typeface provided by Comicraft/Active Images.

Library of Congress Cataloging-in-Publication Data

Schweizer, Chris.
     Tricky Coyote tales / by Chris Schweizer ; illustrated by Chad Thomas.
       p. cm. — (Tricky journeys)
     Summary: Coyote seeks food and fun in the canyons and hills of the southwest, and the reader helps him make choices as he encounters many other creatures, some friendly and some dangerous.
     ISBN: 978–0–7613–6601–0 (lib. bdg. : alk. paper) 1. Plot-your-own stories. 2. Graphic novels. [1. Coyote (Legendary character)—Fiction. 2. Tricksters—Fiction. 3. Animals—Fiction. 4. Plot-your-own stories.] I. Thomas, Chad, ill. II. Title.
PZ7.7.S39Tqc 2011
741.5'973—dc22   2010050871

Manufactured in the United States of America
2 – CG – 5/1/12

Are you ready for your Tricky Journeys™?

You'll find yourself right smack in the middle of this story's tricks, jokes, thrills, and fun.

Each page tells what happens to Coyote and his friends. **YOU** get to decide what happens next. Read each page until you reach a choice. Then pick the choice **YOU** like best.

But be careful . . . one wrong choice could land Coyote in a mess even he can't trick his way out of!

Coyote stands on the edge of a big cliff, holding his hands out in front of him. "Easy, friend," he says. A big, nervous-looking grin spreads across his face. "Can we talk about this?"

Coyote's grin LOOKS nervous because Coyote IS nervous. Behind him is a long drop into a raging river. In front of him is a very big, very angry bear. The bear rises up on two legs and bellows loudly enough to blow Coyote's ears back.

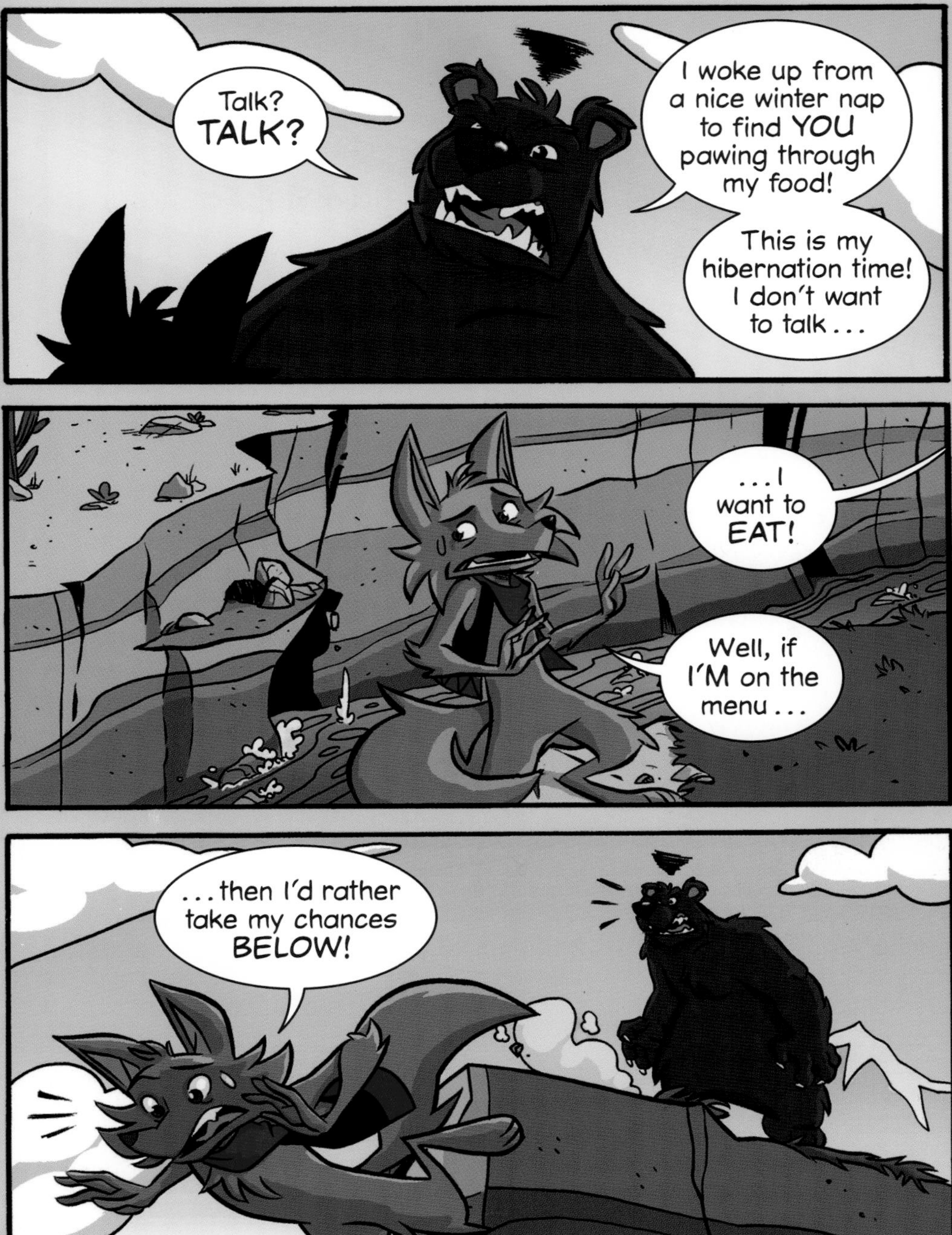
Talk? TALK?
I woke up from a nice winter nap to find YOU pawing through my food!
This is my hibernation time! I don't want to talk . . .
. . . I want to EAT!
Well, if I'M on the menu . . .
. . . then I'd rather take my chances BELOW!

Coyote is falling through the air. He'd better think fast if he wants a safe landing!

If Coyote tries to splash down in the deepest part of the river,

TURN TO PAGE **30.**

If Coyote tries to grab a ledge on the other side,

TURN TO PAGE **46.**

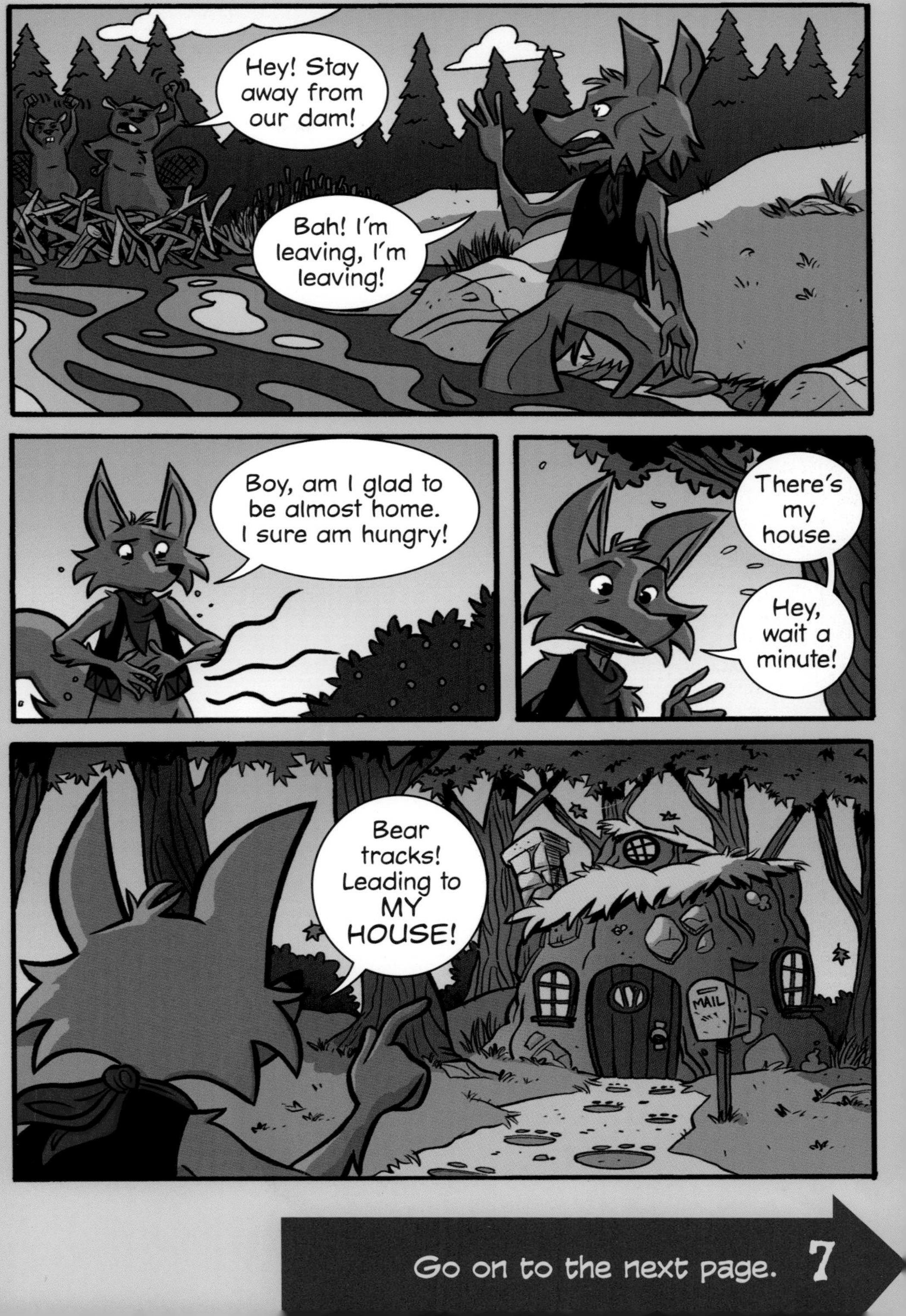
Hey! Stay away from our dam!
Bah! I'm leaving, I'm leaving!
Boy, am I glad to be almost home. I sure am hungry!
There's my house.
Hey, wait a minute!
Bear tracks! Leading to MY HOUSE!
MAIL

Go on to the next page.

"Did the bear come back here to get me?" Coyote wonders. "I sure don't want to run into him . . . but I don't want him hiding in my house, either!"

If Coyote runs away as fast as he can,

TURN TO PAGE 24.

If Coyote goes into his house,

TURN TO PAGE 55.

Coyote grabs the fish's tail. "Hey! Let go!" says the fish. The fish takes off, dragging Coyote behind him!

With a splash and a jump, Coyote and the salmon are flying through the air. Coyote lets go and falls onto the muddy riverbank.

The salmon pops his head above the water. "No one grabs MY tail!" he says. "Have fun trying to survive OUT OF THE WATER, mister!" He swims away.

Coyote hears laughing. It's a little prairie dog. "He thought you were a fish too!" says the prairie dog.

"So, you think that's funny?" asks Coyote. "What are you doing by the river anyway?"

Go on to the next page. 9

"I'm trying to find help for our annual coal party!" says the prairie dog.

Coyote's still very hungry. The little prairie dog might taste good. But a party usually has lots of snacks!

If Coyote tries to trick the prairie dog so that he can eat it,

TURN TO PAGE 62.

If Coyote offers to help with the coal party,

TURN TO PAGE 27.

10

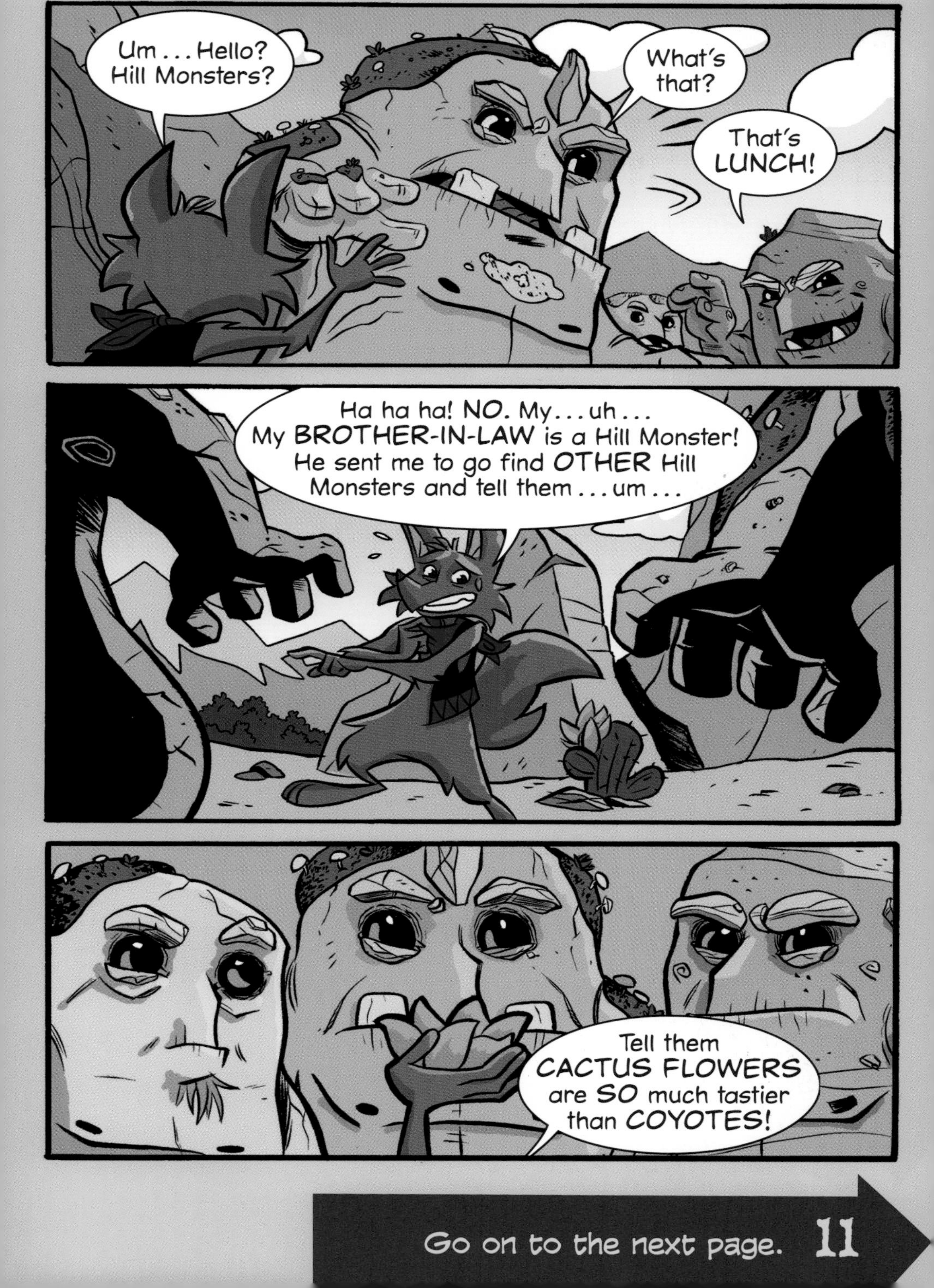
Um . . . Hello? Hill Monsters?
What's that?
That's LUNCH!
Ha ha ha! NO. My . . . uh . . . My BROTHER-IN-LAW is a Hill Monster! He sent me to go find OTHER Hill Monsters and tell them . . . um . . .
Tell them CACTUS FLOWERS are SO much tastier than COYOTES!

The Hill Monsters give Coyote a mean look.

If Coyote tries to run away,

TURN TO PAGE **33**.

If Coyote tries to convince the Hill Monsters not to eat him,

TURN TO PAGE **51**.

Coyote uses the last of his strength to flop over onto the cliff top. He lies on his back to catch his breath.

"Coyote!" comes a deep roar. Standing in front of him is the huge bear. The bear reaches out and grabs him!

"I thought you'd been hurt in that fall!" says the bear. The bear is hugging him, not crushing him! "I was mad because I had to chase you out before I got to eat my snack. But I was not mad enough to want you to fall into the river!" The bear picks Coyote up. "How can I make it up to you?"

Coyote smiles. "Maybe we can share that snack?"

THE END

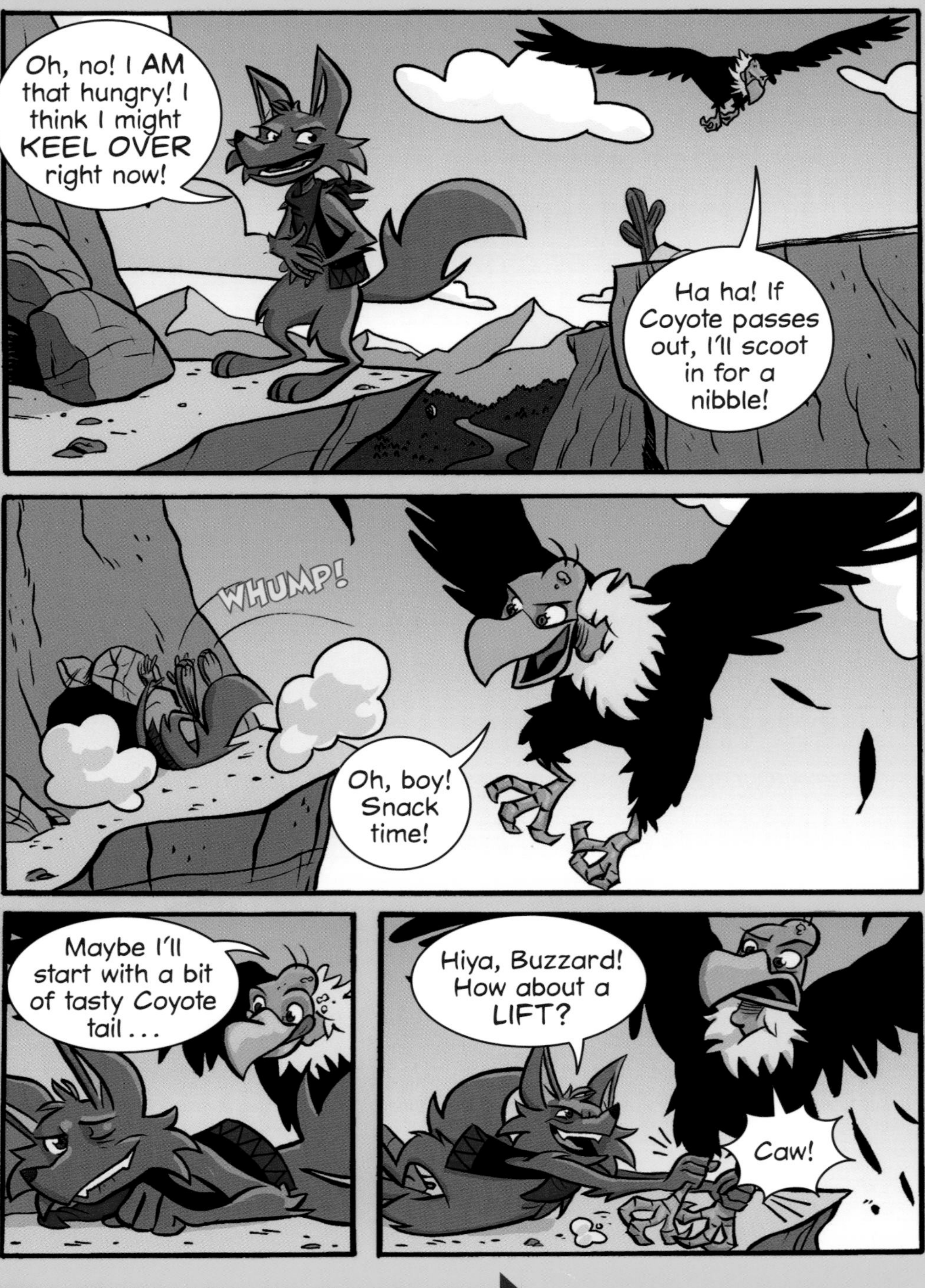
Oh, no! I AM that hungry! I think I might KEEL OVER right now!
Ha ha! If Coyote passes out, I'll scoot in for a nibble!
WHUMP!
Oh, boy! Snack time!
Maybe I'll start with a bit of tasty Coyote tail . . .
Hiya, Buzzard! How about a LIFT?
Caw!

Go on to the next page.

Buzzard flaps his wings, trying to shake Coyote off, but Coyote holds on firmly. Soon they're flying high above the river. "Let go, you trickster!" yells Buzzard.

"I won't let go until we're a long way from that bear!" says Coyote. "There's a forest over to the east. Maybe I can find some dinner there!"

Buzzard shakes his head. "You'd have better luck in prairie dog village, just west of here. They're about to have their big feast! But they don't much like outsiders."

Go on to the next page.

Coyote's stomach is rumbling so loud that the critters below think it's a thunderstorm! He needs to find some food.

If he steers Buzzard toward the forest,

TURN TO PAGE 34.

If he goes to the prairie dog village,

TURN TO PAGE 61.

"You've got the wrong guy," Coyote says. "I'm no trickster!"

"Good!" says the giant bird. "I'd never let a trickster anywhere NEAR my nest." The bird picks up Coyote with her giant beak. She starts walking toward a CHEEP CHEEP sound.

They stop in front of a nest full of baby birds—but the babies are much bigger than Coyote!

The giant bird drops Coyote into the nest. "Wait!" calls Coyote. "I'm trapped in here!"

"Of course," says the big bird. "My babies couldn't eat if their dinner could just run away!"

The baby birds cheep as they hop toward Coyote, and he knows that for him, this is

THE END

So it's TRUE!

A STRANGER! In our NEST!

Wait... WHAT'S true?

That you three have the most beautiful jackets in the world! ALMOST.

Almost? ALMOST?!

Did you come here to INSULT us?

No, no!

I'm Coyote, the world-famous jacket artist!

I came to offer my services.

One word: STRIPES. All the best-dressed wasps have them these days.

Ooh! Me FIRST!

No, ME!

I'M oldest. I go first!

Easy, easy! I'll paint all your jackets at once!

"Lie down, and I'll paint your backs," says Coyote. The sisters lie down, and Coyote uses ash and water to mix up a dye. Using the stick, he paints one stripe, then another, then another.

"Now I'LL have the most beautiful coat," says one sister. They all start arguing again.

"Nobody move," says Coyote, "or the stripes will smudge. I'll wait outside." But first, he holds his stick in the fireplace until the end catches on fire.

He steps out of the nest and walks to where the prairie dog is waiting. "Let's go start that feast," says Coyote, and away they run.

THE END

"I've squeezed through tighter spots than that!" Coyote exclaims. He dives into the hole . . .

. . . almost. His hips get wedged in the opening! Coyote strains and struggles, but he can't get loose!

Coyote hears chattering coming from deeper in the hole and freezes. Maybe it's someone who can help. Then again, maybe it's someone who might take advantage of Coyote's situation.

As his eyes get used to the darkness, Coyote can see what is making the chattering noise. It's a group of moles!

If Coyote tries to trick the moles into helping him get free,

TURN TO PAGE 40.

If Coyote tries to stay perfectly still in the hopes that the moles won't notice him,

TURN TO PAGE 25.

21

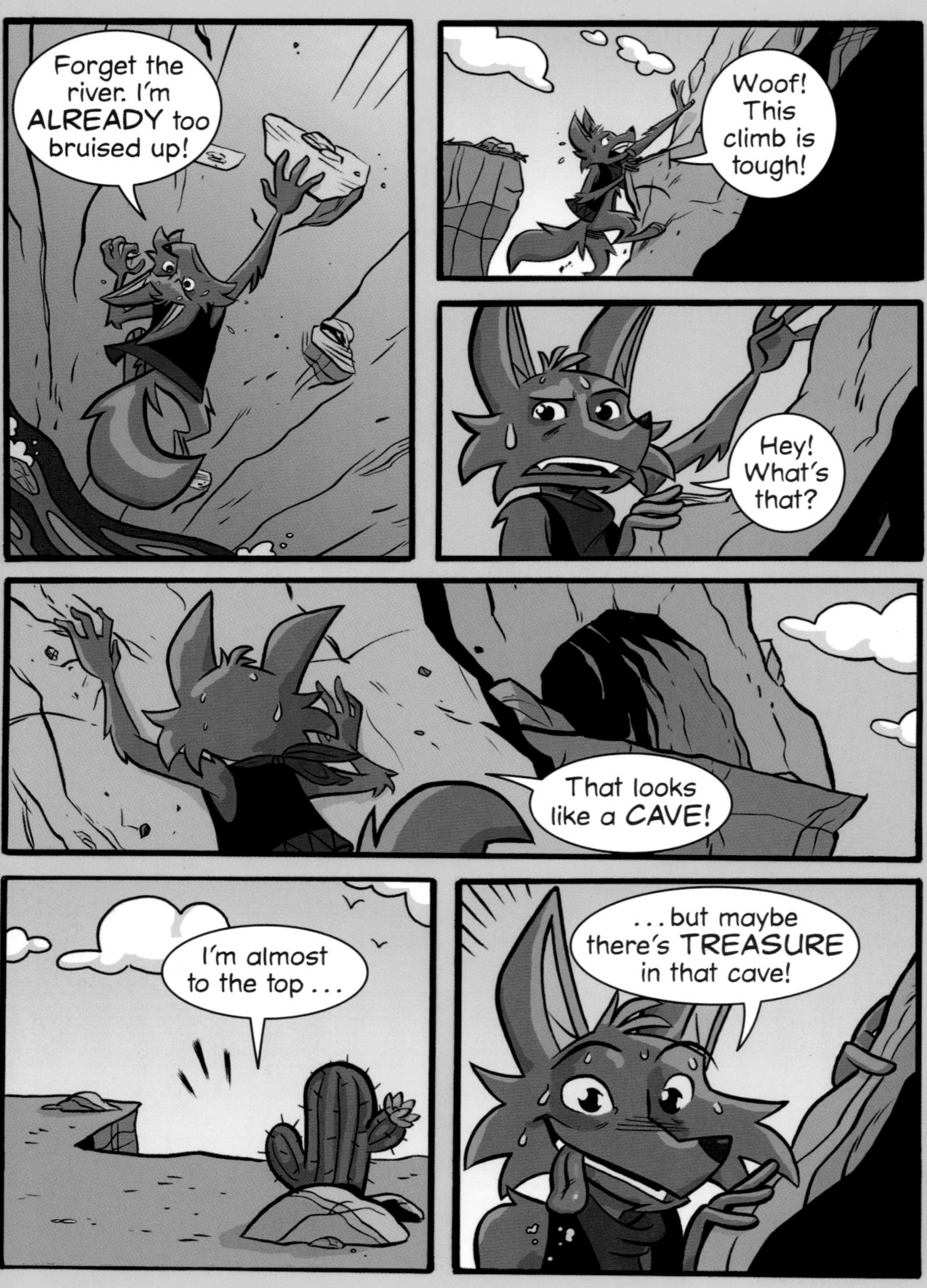
Forget the river. I'm ALREADY too bruised up!
Woof! This climb is tough!
Hey! What's that?
That looks like a CAVE!
I'm almost to the top . . .
. . . but maybe there's TREASURE in that cave!

Go on to the next page.

"I might be too tired to climb over there," Coyote says. "I would love to get out of this canyon and head for home." He looks back at the cave. "It sure would be nice, though, if my home was stuffed to the roof with treasure!"

If Coyote climbs to the top,

TURN TO PAGE 13.

If Coyote tries to climb over to the cave,

TURN TO PAGE 59.

"I don't want to run into that bear again!" says Coyote. He turns around and runs . . .

. . . right into the bear!

"Your house was too small for me, so I thought I'd wait out here," growls the bear. With a mighty paw, he sticks Coyote under his big, hairy arm. "I'm taking you back to my cave, and if I'm not too hungry, I'll teach you some manners."

Coyote tries to wiggle away, but the bear is too strong. "I think I AM too hungry," the bear says. He licks his lips, and Coyote realizes that for him, this is

THE END

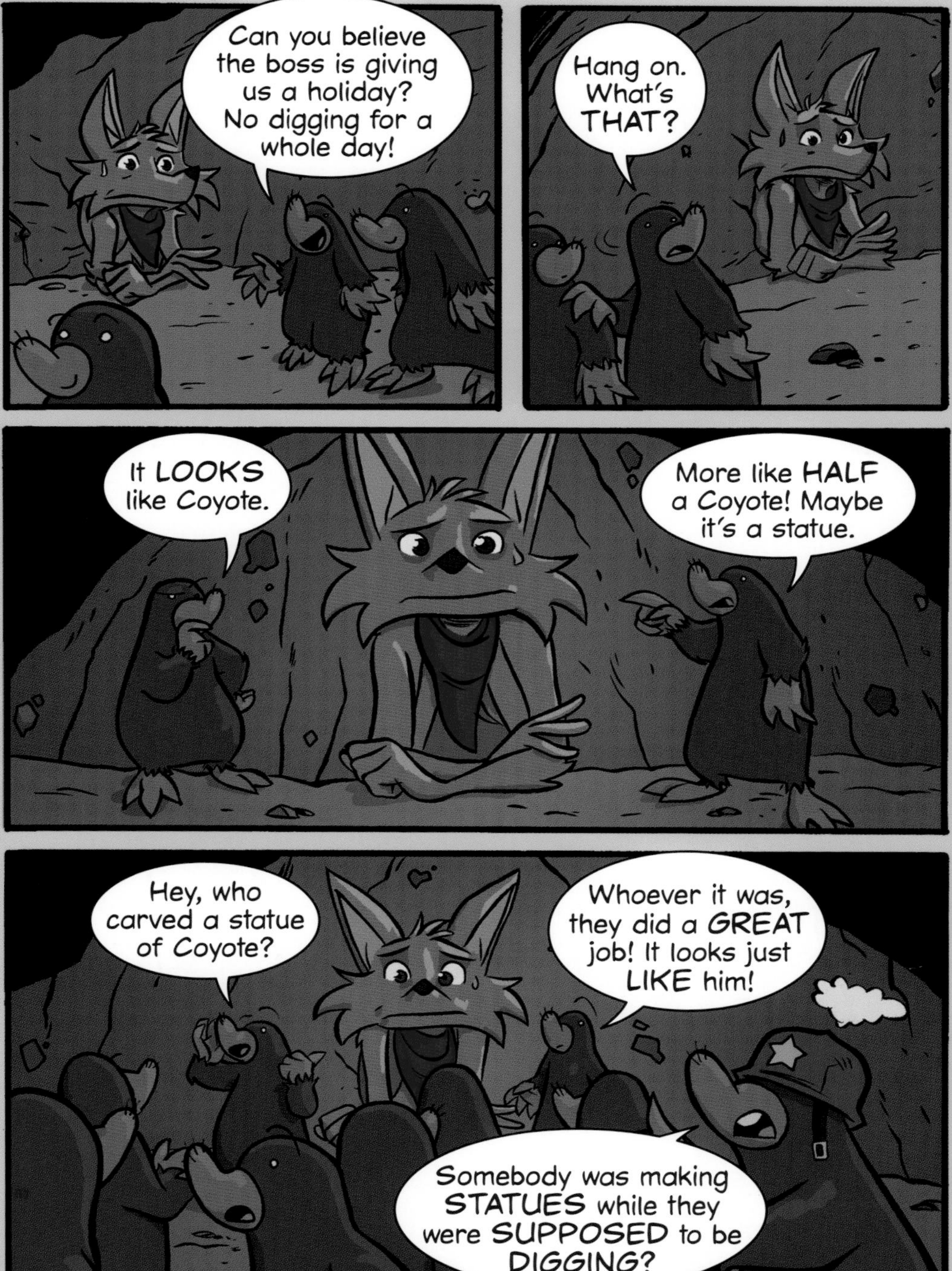
Can you believe the boss is giving us a holiday? No digging for a whole day!
Hang on. What's THAT?
It LOOKS like Coyote.
More like HALF a Coyote! Maybe it's a statue.
Hey, who carved a statue of Coyote?
Whoever it was, they did a GREAT job! It looks just LIKE him!
Somebody was making STATUES while they were SUPPOSED to be DIGGING?

Go on to the next page.

"That's it!" cries the boss mole, storming away down a tunnel. "Because of that statue, the holiday is canceled!"

The other moles stomp the ground. "We haven't had a holiday all year!" says one.

"When I find out who put this statue here, I'll tie his snout in a knot and bury him upside down in mud!" says another. They sit down grumbling in front of Coyote.

Coyote knows that he'd better stay perfectly still as long as the moles are around. He made them lose their holiday! He doesn't want them to turn their anger on him.

Looks like he's going to be stuck for a long time!

THE END

I'd be HAPPY to help! What's a coal party?

It's a big feast where we roast all our food!

We want to roast the food, but we don't have any FIRE.

How did you get fire for your OTHER coal parties?

OTHER coal parties? This will be the FIRST ONE!

The YELLOW JACKET SISTERS have fire, but they're the meanest critters around. They would NEVER share!

Go on to the next page. **27**

"I saw a fellow make fire once," says Coyote. "I might be able to do it myself. But I sure don't like it when folks are mean. Maybe we should teach those Yellow Jacket Sisters a lesson in sharing!"

If Coyote tries to make fire himself,

TURN TO PAGE 56.

If he tries to get it from the Yellow Jacket Sisters,

TURN TO PAGE 42.

"Mercy me!" cries one of the beavers as Coyote swims up to their dam. "We saw you bouncing off those rocks. You poor dear! Come on inside. We'll get you warmed up!"

The beavers help Coyote out of the water and into their lodge. "Here you go, dear," says one beaver, handing him some soup.

"You look like you've had a very rough day!" says the other beaver.

"Oh, I have," says Coyote, "but it's a lot better now!"

THE END

29

Coyote curls up into a ball. He hits the water below with a SPLASH so big that the bear's fur gets soaked all the way up on the cliff top. "COYOTE!" the bear roars.

The river rapids swirl around Coyote. He tries to swim, but he bounces off one big rock and then another. "These rocks are going to pulverize me!" he thinks.

He sees a flat stone up ahead at a fork in the river. Just as he's about to be swept past, he grabs on and pulls himself onto the slippery surface.

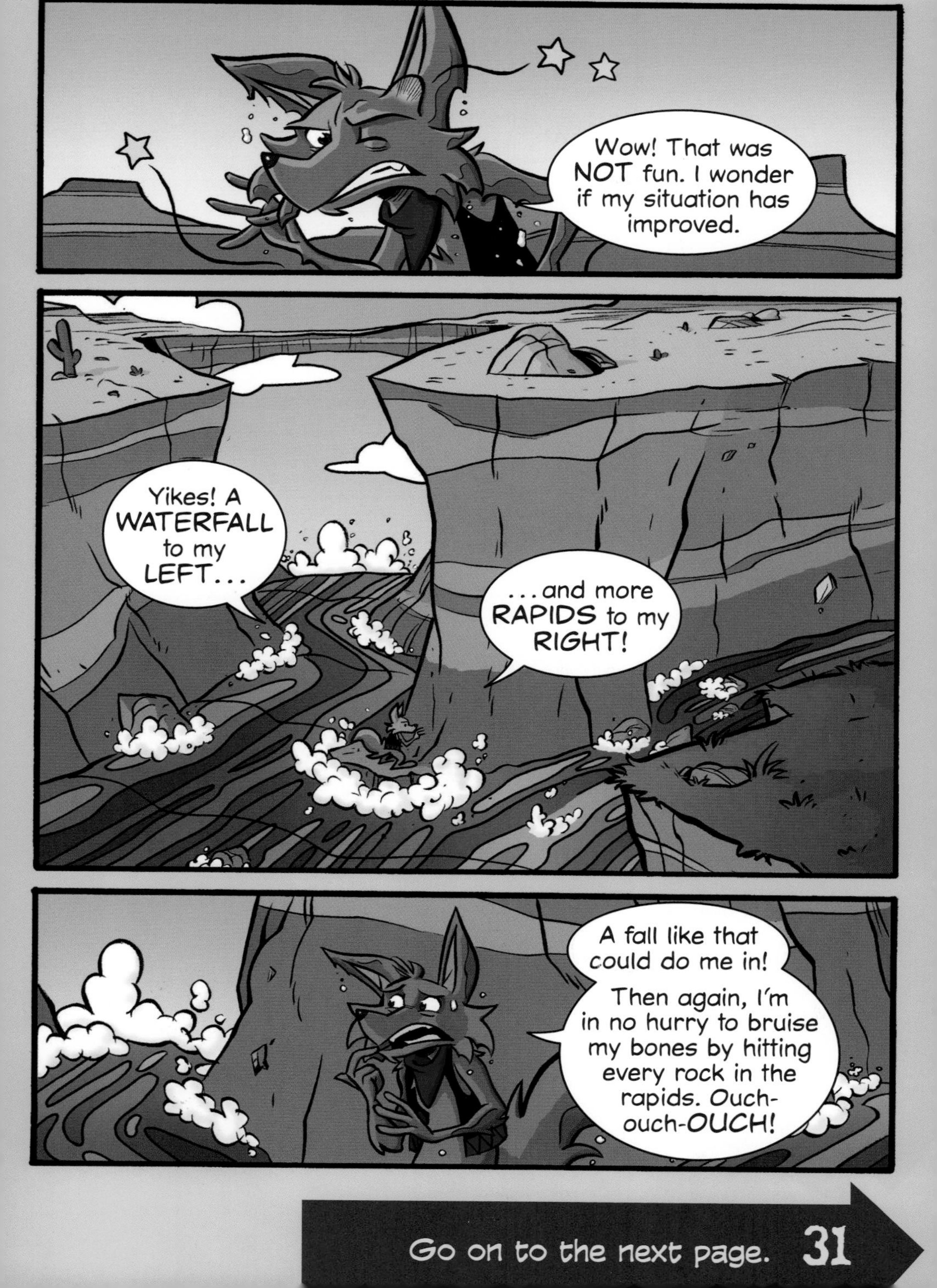
Wow! That was NOT fun. I wonder if my situation has improved.
Yikes! A WATERFALL to my LEFT...
...and more RAPIDS to my RIGHT!
A fall like that could do me in!
Then again, I'm in no hurry to bruise my bones by hitting every rock in the rapids. Ouch-ouch-OUCH!

Coyote is already pretty sore!

If he lets the waterfall carry him over,

TURN TO PAGE 53.

If he tries to swim to safety through the rapids,

TURN TO PAGE 49.

If he tries to climb the ravine wall,

TURN TO PAGE 22.

Coyote drops the flower and jumps over the baby. He runs away as fast as he can. He can hear the Hill Monsters roaring behind him, but they're slow and clumsy. He comes to the edge of the ledge, but he has a running start.

He jumps and with a loud THUD lands on the other side. He climbs up the rocks and stands proudly on top of the cliff. "Looks like I won't be anyone's lunch today!" he calls to the Hill Monsters.

"Oh, I wouldn't say THAT," says a deep growl.

The bear is standing right behind him. Poor Coyote. He knows that this is

THE END

No, sir! It's the **FOREST** for me! Put me near those treetops, and I'll let go of your legs.

Thanks, Buzzard!

WHUMP!

What an old **TRICKSTER!**

Hey, you! This is **SQUIRREL'S** tree!

Um . . . what luck! I was **LOOKING** for you!

Really? For ME?

"You're the squirrel who hides nuts in the tree, yes?" Coyote asks.

The squirrel frowns. "All squirrels do that!"

Coyote pats the squirrel on the head. "I'M looking for a squirrel who is very clever," he says.

"I'm clever!" says the squirrel, jumping up and down. "You MUST be looking for ME!"

"That's right!" says Coyote. "I've come to warn you. One of the nuts you've hidden tastes like . . . SKUNK JUICE!"

"Oh, no!" says the squirrel. "How do I know which one?"

Coyote smiles. "I'll be happy to eat each one until we find the bad nut!" he says.

"Oh, how brave!" says the squirrel. "I'll go and get them!" Coyote licks his lips. He is going to have as many nuts as he can eat!

THE END

Coyote waves and points. "Oh, you want to get out!" says the salmon. "We can help. Come on, everybody!"

Coyote is lifted by a big school of fish until he's at the surface! He takes a breath. Then he's hit hard by the falling river.

The salmon bounce him from nose to nose as they try to swim UP THE WATERFALL! "Don't worry," says one of the salmon. "It's slow, but we'll get to the top by next week! We're going home, but we are glad to take you along with us!"

All day, Coyote is painfully bumped from salmon to salmon. It's going to be a long week!

THE END

Hmmm . . . If this ledge wraps around, I might be able to find a way up!

Oh, no!

Hill Monsters!

I'll just turn around and . . .

WAAA!

WAAA!

Oh, no! A Hill Monster BABY!

Go on to the next page. 37

If the Hill Monsters look to see what is making the baby cry, they'll catch Coyote on the ledge.

If Coyote tries to get the baby to stop crying,

TURN TO PAGE **58.**

If Coyote pretends he isn't scared of the Hill Monsters,

TURN TO PAGE **11.**

Coyote tiptoes a little closer to the fire and holds the tip of the stick in it. The wood crackles as it catches on fire, and the giant wasps spin around when they hear the noise. One flies between Coyote and the door.

"So," she says, "another little mammal is trying to steal our fire!" The other sisters buzz angrily. Coyote backs up against the wall of the nest. The sisters start to fly slowly toward him, their giant stingers pointed and ready to strike.

THE END

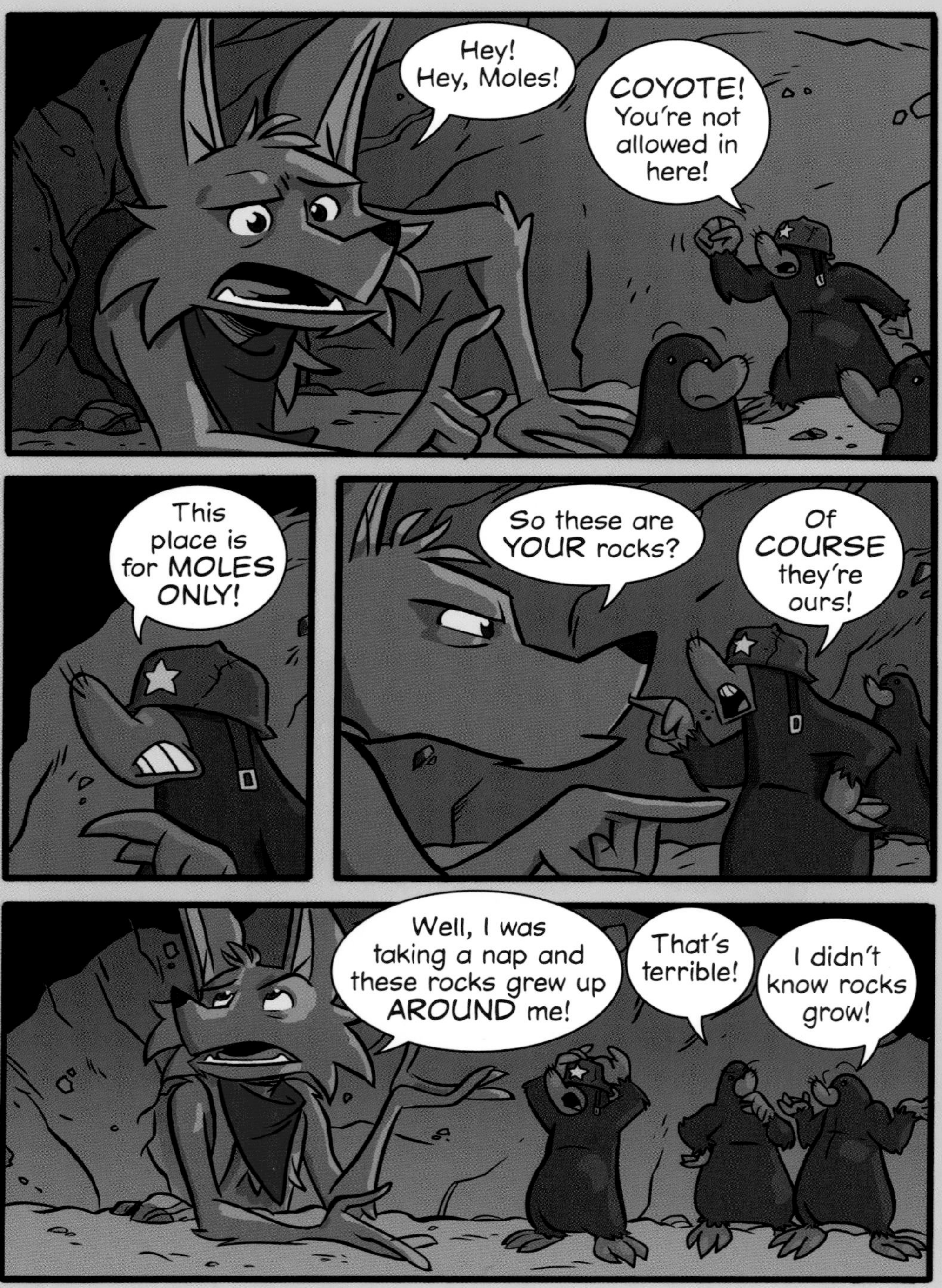
Hey!
Hey, Moles!
COYOTE! You're not allowed in here!
This place is for MOLES ONLY!
So these are YOUR rocks?
Of COURSE they're ours!
Well, I was taking a nap and these rocks grew up AROUND me!
That's terrible!
I didn't know rocks grow!

Go on to the next page.

"We'll dig you out of there, Coyote!" says one of the moles. The other moles nod. They start clawing away at the crumbly rock.

After a few minutes, there's enough room for Coyote to wiggle free. He rolls into the cave. The moles take him by the paw.

"Come, Coyote," they say. "Let us give you a big dinner to make amends for the behavior of our terrible rocks."

"If that will make you feel better," he says, "let's eat!"

THE END

The prairie dog leads Coyote to the nest where the Yellow Jacket Sisters live. It's huge! And these bugs are as big as Coyote is!

Inside, the three sisters have a fire burning in a small fireplace. They're looking into a mirror.

"I think my jacket is the most beautiful," says one.

"That is ridiculous," says another. "Mine is clearly the most beautiful. Look how yellow it is!"

"You're both wrong," says the third. "Mine is without question the most beautiful jacket in the world."

The sisters are so busy arguing, they don't even see Coyote walk over to the fireplace.

Coyote takes a stick out of the woodpile beside the fireplace. If he's lucky, he can make a torch and get out before the sisters notice that he's there. But if they see him, he might not be able to get out safely.

If Coyote tries to sneak away with the fire,

TURN TO PAGE **39.**

If Coyote tries to trick the Yellow Jacket Sisters,

TURN TO PAGE **18.**

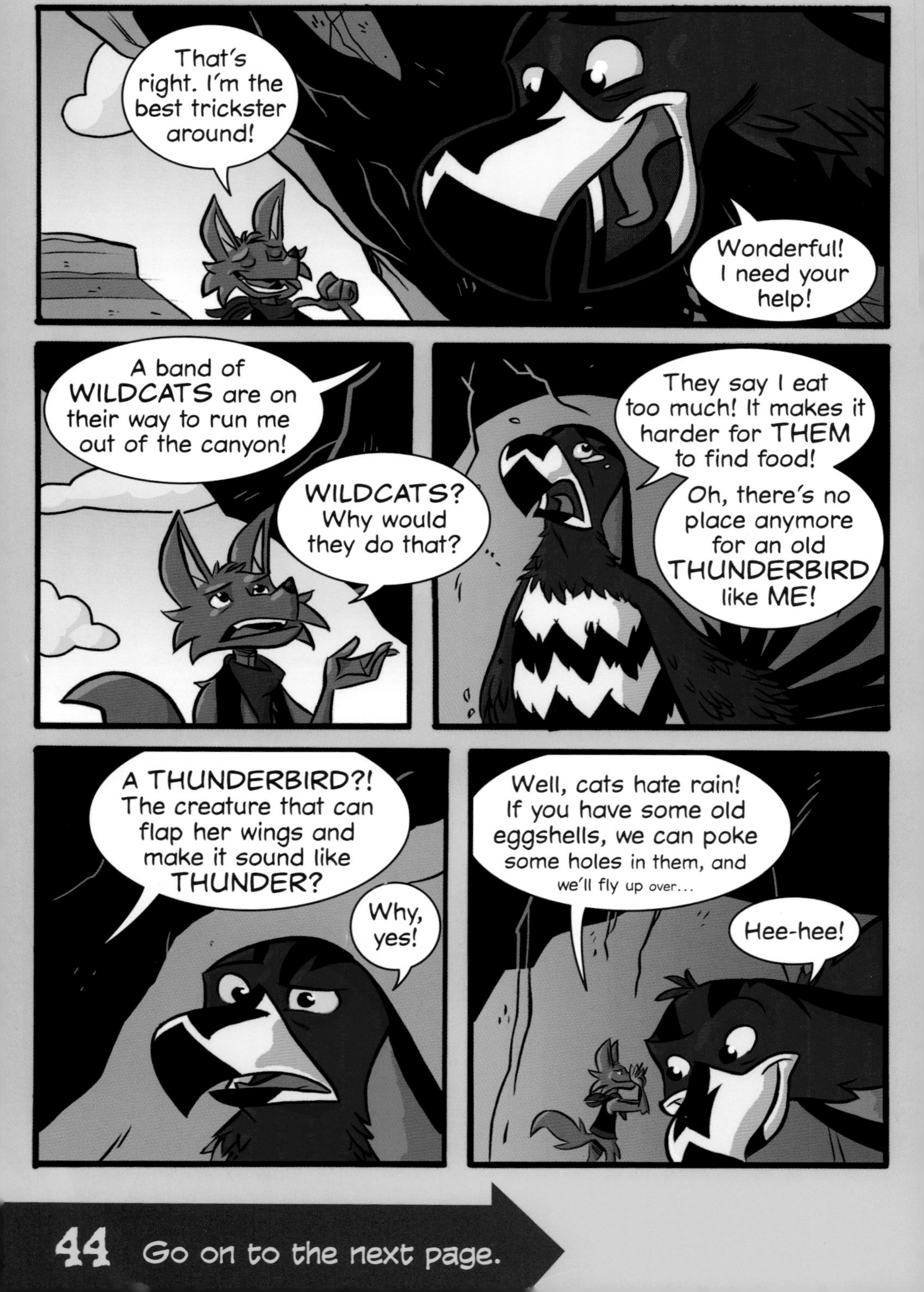
That's right. I'm the best trickster around!
Wonderful! I need your help!
A band of WILDCATS are on their way to run me out of the canyon!
WILDCATS? Why would they do that?
They say I eat too much! It makes it harder for THEM to find food!
Oh, there's no place anymore for an old THUNDERBIRD like ME!
A THUNDERBIRD?! The creature that can flap her wings and make it sound like THUNDER?
Why, yes!
Well, cats hate rain! If you have some old eggshells, we can poke some holes in them, and we'll fly up over...
Hee-hee!

The band of wildcats are on their way across the canyon. There's the sound of thunder, and water starts dripping on their heads. "Oh, no!" says one of them. "It's a storm! We'd better turn back."

"But what about the big old bird?" says another.

"Forget it!" says a third wildcat. "That thunder means more rain is coming." The wildcats run home as fast as they can.

High in the sky, Coyote is riding the Thunderbird's back. "We sure tricked them with this eggshell!" Coyote laughs. "By poking holes in it and filling it with water, we made them think it was raining!" The thunderbird laughs too. With a rumbling flap of her wings, she turns to fly Coyote home.

THE END

THUD!

Oof!

Yikes! That was close!

Coyote!

Don't think you can get away from me so easily!

I'd better make tracks before Bear figures out a way across the ravine!

I'll catch you, Coyote!

"I'll catch you!" the bear roars as he lumbers out of sight.

"Of all the rotten luck," Coyote says. "That bear woke up before I had a chance to eat anything, and I'm still hungry!"

He hears a caw above him and sees a buzzard circling overhead. "Not hungry enough for YOU to be waiting around!" Coyote yells, shaking his fist.

Coyote spots a hole in the rock. It might lead to an interesting cave. But the hole is pretty small. The last thing Coyote wants is to get stuck!

Go on to the next page.

Coyote can't see if the ledge keeps going around the next corner. Coyote could get stuck there for days! Coyote looks at the hole, then the ledge, and then up at the buzzard.

If Coyote tries to squeeze through the hole in the rock,

TURN TO PAGE 20.

If Coyote tries to walk along the ledge,

TURN TO PAGE 37.

If Coyote tries to trick the Buzzard into giving him a ride,

TURN TO PAGE 14.

Better a bunch of rocks than a giant drop!

Ow!

BONK

BONK

Ow!

Ow!

BONK

Finally! I'm out of the canyon, and the river is slowing down.

Uh-oh!

Those BEAVERS have seen me!

Go on to the next page.

"If they're mad, they might try to club me with those flat tails!" Coyote thinks. "Maybe they're friendly...but maybe they're not."

If Coyote talks to the beavers,

TURN TO PAGE
29.

If Coyote swims to the shore and goes into the woods,

TURN TO PAGE
7.

It's delicious!

You're trying to TRICK us!

Hill Monsters CAN'T eat FLOWERS!

Um... Why not?

Because we're HILL MONSTERS! We can't digest PLANTS and--yuck!--VEGETABLES.

They'll turn us to STONE!

That's why we carry around this big sack of beef jerky!

Why waste our JERKY when there's meat right HERE?

Ha!

AAAAAAAAAAAA!

How did he taste?

Delicious!

Go on to the next page.

Suddenly, the Hill Monster's stomach starts to gurgle. He opens his mouth wide and says "Oh, NOOOOO—" Then he turns entirely to stone.

Coyote climbs out the Hill Monster's mouth.

"What happened to our friend?" asks one of the Hill Monsters.

"He tried to eat me," says Coyote, "and I'm a VEGETABLE!" He takes a step toward them, and they scream and jump into the river.

"It's a good thing I was still holding this cactus flower when he popped me in his mouth!" Coyote says to himself. "Otherwise, I'd still be in his belly! Now," he says, scratching his chin. "Where did they leave that jerky?"

THE END

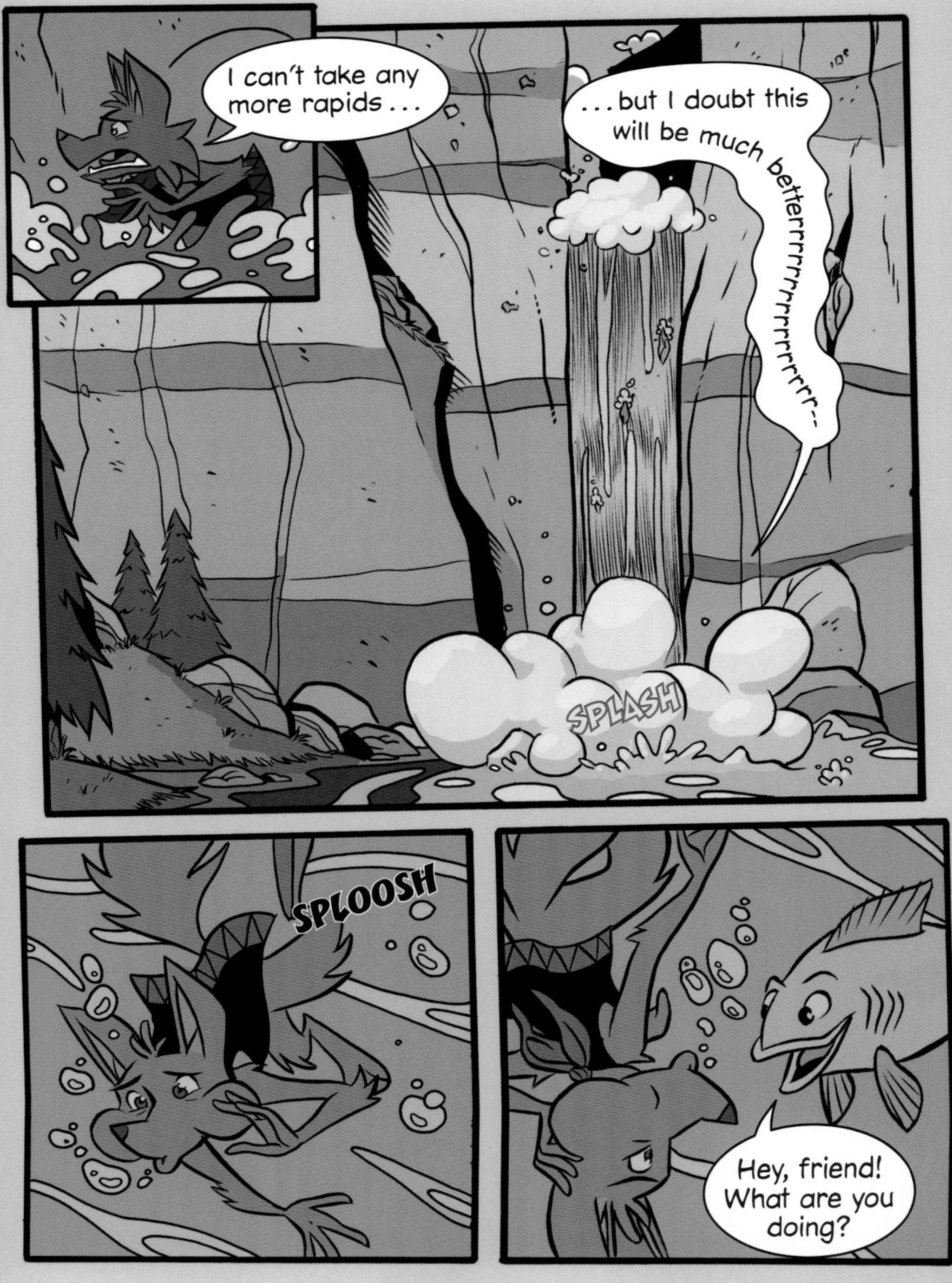
I can't take any more rapids . . .
. . . but I doubt this will be much betterrrrrrrrrrrrrrrrrrrr--
SPLASH
SPLOOSH
Hey, friend! What are you doing?

Go on to the next page.

The water is swirling around Coyote so much that he can't find his way to the surface! Maybe that friendly salmon can help, because Coyote can't hold his breath much longer.

If he asks the salmon for directions,

TURN TO PAGE
36.

If he holds on to the salmon's tail in the hopes it will swim him out of there,

TURN TO PAGE
9.

"That bear might be scary, but nobody keeps me out of my own house!" Coyote opens the door.

"All right, Bear," he says. "Here I am!" But the bear is smiling and bouncing up and down.

"I'm glad you're back!" says the bear. "Please, oh PLEASE teach me how to do that!"

Coyote is confused. "How to do what?" he asks.

"How to make a giant splash!" says the bear, bumping his big head on Coyote's ceiling.

"It's called a cannonball. I'll be happy to teach you," says Coyote. "In fact, I know a couple of beavers who need a good soaking . . ."

THE END

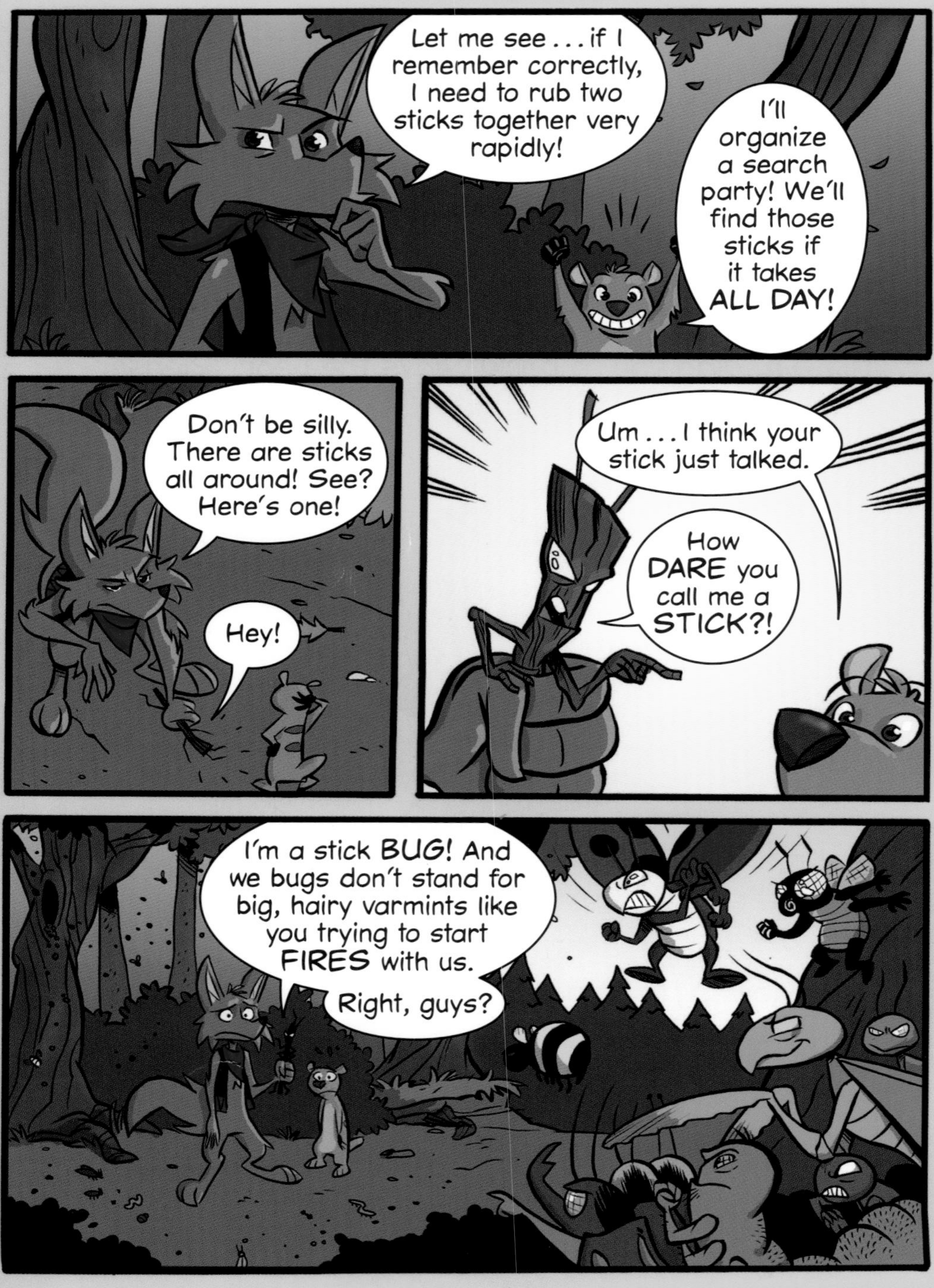
Let me see . . . if I remember correctly, I need to rub two sticks together very rapidly!
I'll organize a search party! We'll find those sticks if it takes ALL DAY!
Don't be silly. There are sticks all around! See? Here's one!
Hey!
Um . . . I think your stick just talked.
How DARE you call me a STICK?!
I'm a stick BUG! And we bugs don't stand for big, hairy varmints like you trying to start FIRES with us.
Right, guys?

Go on to the next page.

Coyote slowly sets the stick bug down on the grass. Hundreds of other bugs come out of their hiding places. "Let's just step back," Coyote tells the prairie dog, "and maybe they'll leave us alone."

But Coyote should have looked where he was going. He steps on a beetle, who yells out angrily, "Hey! Watch it!" All of a sudden, the bugs swarm toward Coyote and the prairie dog. Terrified, Coyote and the prairie dog take off running into the woods.

If there IS a feast, Coyote is going to miss it. He's too busy trying not to get stung or bitten to think about food, anyway!

THE END

"My mother used to hold out her FINGER for me to suck on when I was a baby," Coyote thinks. "That would get ME to stop crying!"

Sure enough, when Coyote holds out his finger, the baby puts it in its mouth. The baby stops crying. Coyote looks up to see if the Hill Monsters have turned around, but so far, none have. He looks back at the baby . . .

. . . and sees that his whole arm is in the baby's mouth! He tries to pull it out, but the hungry baby gives another big hungry slurp, and for Coyote, that is

THE END

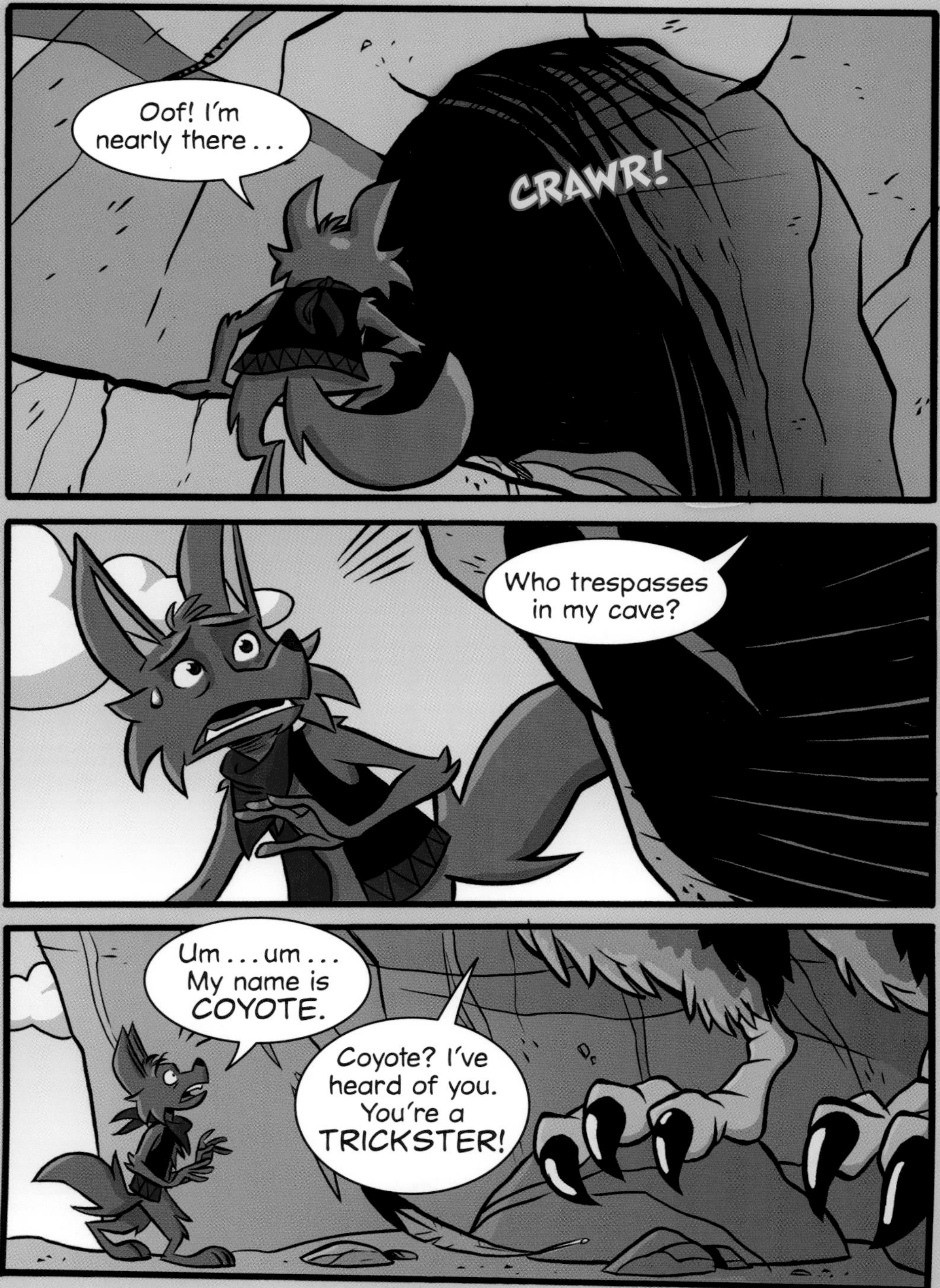
Oof! I'm nearly there . . .
CRAWR!
Who trespasses in my cave?
Um . . . um . . . My name is COYOTE.
Coyote? I've heard of you. You're a TRICKSTER!

Go on to the next page.

"Who, me?" Coyote says, looking up at the biggest, scariest bird that he has ever seen. Maybe Coyote can trick his way to freedom. Then again, maybe Coyote should tell the truth.

If Coyote denies being a trickster,

TURN TO PAGE
17.

If Coyote admits to being a trickster,

TURN TO PAGE
44.

Buzzard flies to where hundreds of little prairie dogs are dancing around a fire. Coyote drops and lands right in the middle of the group. "Howdy, gang!" he says, waving at all of them. "I hear you're having a feast."

The prairie dogs look at one another, then look at Coyote. "The feast comes AFTER the big hunt," says one of the prairie dogs.

"What do you hunt?" Coyote asks, licking his lips at the thought of dinner.

They raise their spears and point them at Coyote. "It's different each year," the prairie dogs say. "This year, we're hunting COYOTE."

THE END

What kind of help do you need?

We need help to sing the COAL SONG!

"The coal song"?

To celebrate the coming winter, we prairie dogs bury ourselves in hot coals.

OUCH! Doesn't that HURT?

Not if we sing the COAL SONG! It makes us FIREPROOF, and the coals feel warm and comfortable! It goes, "Hey-hee-hi, hee-hi-hoo, hey-yah-hey-yah hoo!"

We take turns singing, so that everyone has a chance to lie in the coals!

If I sing, you can all lie under the coals together!

You would do that for US?

How generous!

Coyote starts to sing, and the prairie dogs burrow under the hot coals. Then Coyote stops singing!

"Ouch! Ouch!" cry the prairie dogs. "If you don't sing the song, we're not fireproof!"

Coyote laughs. "I want you to be baked by the coals so I can eat you up!" he says.

But the prairie dogs start climbing out! "We aren't fireproof, but we can still move!" they yell. They pick up the hot coals and start throwing them at Coyote. Coyote runs off into the woods.

He won't find any food here, and he'll be in big trouble if those prairie dogs catch him!

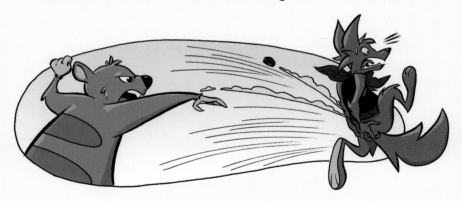

THE END

COYOTE is a huge part of Native American folklore in North America. Usually in these stories, he is a trickster, but sometimes he is a helper of humanity, doing things like stealing fire for us to use. He is also thought to be responsible for the way a number of animals look today.

The story of the prairie dogs getting trapped in the coals because Coyote stops singing a magic song comes from the Lakota tribe. This story is meant to explain why prairie dogs have what look like grill markings on their backs. The story of Coyote stealing fire from the Yellow Jackets and painting stripes on them comes from the Karuk tribe of California.

In some stories, Coyote fights monsters! He turns them to stone. In one Apache story, he is eaten by a baby monster! A story sometimes even has different endings depending on who tells it—just like in this book!